Follow the River

by LYDIA DABCOVICH

A Unicorn Book • E. P. Dutton • New York

Copyright © 1980 by Lydia Dabcovich

Library of Congress Cataloging in Publication Data

Dabcovich, Lydia. Follow the river.
(A Unicorn book)
Summary: Follows a stream from its home in the mountains
through the countryside where it becomes a river and
eventually flows into the ocean.
[1. Rivers—Fiction] I. Title.
PZ7.D12Fo [E] 80-10173 ISBN: 0-525-30015-5

Published in the United States by E. P. Dutton, a Division
of Elsevier-Dutton Publishing Company, Inc., New York

Published simultaneously in Canada by Clarke,
Irwin & Company Limited, Toronto and Vancouver

Editor: Emilie McLeod   Designer: Claire Counihan

Printed in the U.S.A.   First Edition
10 9 8 7 6 5 4 3 2 1

for Mu and Tabe

High up in the mountains
a little stream
starts on its way down

through thick woods.
The little stream
is joined by other streams.
It grows deeper and wider
until it is a river.

Down again it falls
over big rocks,
splashy and foamy.
The river rushes on

by a mill

and around an island,

under a bridge

and by a village,

past an old town on a hill

and through a big city.

Rain falls into the river

and sunshine warms it.

The river moves through nights

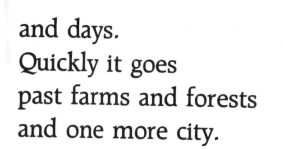

and days.
Quickly it goes
past farms and forests
and one more city.

The river widens
into a busy harbor

and carries boats
out into the sea.